AF379449

Sarah Read has been teaching English for seven years in and around the counties of Wiltshire and Gloucestershire.

Her passion for her subject inspired her to write *Shadowlands* a short fictional story aimed at engaging hesitant readers in fiction again. The novel is the first in the *Descent into Chaos* trilogy.

She lives in Wiltshire with her Husband and their growing collection of rock climbing equipment.

SHADOWLANDS

This book is dedicated to my friends and family, but especially to Aaron Read – thank you for your unfailing belief in my dreams.

Sarah Read

SHADOWLANDS

AUSTIN MACAULEY
PUBLISHERS LTD.

ISBN 978 184963 394 9

www.austinmacauley.com

First Published (2013)
Austin Macauley Publishers Ltd.
25 Canada Square
Canary Wharf
London
E14 5LB

Printed and Bound in Great Britain

Simone. I need you. We need you.

Toil

A gentle breeze blew the blue scarf from out under her Horthari work cap. She panicked; without it she would be punished, deemed naked. The fear fluttered through her as the material passed through her outstretched fingers and skittered off over the field. She threw down the hanodi and ran after it, the scarf teasing her, always just out of her grasp... Her work forgotten... The scarf her only aim... She caught it... The fear passed out from her mouth in a smile of triumph.

In her efforts to catch the missing article of clothing, the girl had failed to notice that the breeze had dropped and disappeared; that the icicles had begun to creep their way across the newly-turned brown soil.

She was oblivious to the frost dragging its way towards her. Her entire attention was focused on the task of reattaching the scarf without revealing the crown of her head, ensuring that all her hair was covered. She tucked the final strand of material into place and turned to retrace her steps, and stopped. Frozen. Rooted to the ground. They were here. They surrounded her. She had no escape. She felt their cold grasp on her hand, and saw the field, the workers and the vivid blue of the sky recede into darkness.

Simone had witnessed the girl's senseless dash after her loosened scarf; had known from the moment that it had fallen that she was lost. She watched with lowered gaze the arrival of the Shadow Keepers, and said a silent prayer to the Hathanoi as they whisked the victim away. At one time, she would have cried for the senseless loss of yet another soul, but the takings had become such a part of life that now all she did was retrieve the abandoned hanodi, the only clue

that the girl had even been there, and returned to her own
toil.

Hathonia

The city bell tolled the end of the working day. The thin line of field and farm workers began to wind their way back towards the safety of the city walls, towards homes, families and the fires that kept the Shadows at bay.

Alexis waited anxiously at the top of the city gate. He hated staying behind in the relative safety of Hathonia whilst Simone went out to the fields, but he had been selected to work for the Elders and to serve the Hathanoi, a calling that could never be denied or walked away from.

The smooth stone of the wall felt cold under his tense grasp. He thought back over the generations of Hathoni who had stood watch over their returning loved ones; had they lived their lives in fear as he did now? Had they watched anxiously for a certain colour of scarf, a particular walk or a secret sign that they had come home, that they had survived a day in the fields?

The black smoke drifted over the column of workers, signifying that someone had been lost to the Shadows. His pulse quickened. He scanned more urgently, looking for her, willing her to still be present in the land of the living.

A small movement caught his eye. He sighed with relief; the purple shimmer of a scarf and the swaying walk let him know she was still here, still Simone, still his.

She passed through the city gates and felt the familiar rush of calm surround her. Hathonia was her home, her sanctuary, and she knew that if asked she would defend it with her life.

Simone knew that Alexis was standing on the gateway above her, she'd be able to see him later once she'd returned her tools to the Guardians. The signs above her reminded all the workers of the reason they put their lives in jeopardy each and every day: 'food, freedom, strength'.

The Elders had started the campaign at a time when the population had been beaten and trodden into submission by the marauding Yetheni, the bitter winter, and the ever-present fear of the Shadow Keepers. It was an idea that formed into a movement; a dedicated team of workers who wanted to provide for their homeland, ensure the survival of their loved ones and keep the hunger away from the city. The ones left behind within the safety of the walls also strived to make the great city safer. The different groups of cleaners, servers, food preparers and general city maintainers were directed to 'clean, cleanse, and strengthen' the buildings and population, by turning the wares that the workers returned with into food and building materials.

Simone knew that by the efforts of the Hathoni they had progressed further than she had ever imagined from the dark days when everything had seemed so hopeless. The arrival of Yessin – the grand advisor to the Elders – had heralded a time of change; of belief that they could be better, that even one day they could escape from the clutches of the Shadow Keepers and emerge into a new existence, free from fear of the darkness that always chased their waking moments, and haunted their dreams.

The Guardian accepted her handoi, and also made a note of the spare that Simone handed over. She didn't need to explain about the loss of the girl. The Guardian had seen the smoke, and understood the connotations of being handed two handois by one worker. He smiled sympathetically and signed Simone's name off on the list.

That night, as they sat in their quarters discussing the day, bathed in the warmth of the firelight, Simone felt a chill creep over her. The unfamiliar feeling that she was being watched in her own home began to eat away at her consciousness.

Alexis noticed her discomfort.

'What is it?'

He anxiously brushed her newly uncovered hair from her face.

'Nothing – just an odd feeling, like we're not alone.'

The flames had steadily been flickering over the wall, but at Simone's voice they blazed in intensity.

'Simone. I need you. We need you.'

Alexis and Simone stared at each other.

'Did you...?'

'Yes, I heard it.'

The fire had returned to its steady stream of flame, acting as though nothing out of the ordinary had occurred, but it had. Their lives had altered from the course that they had been on. They'd heard the voices. They had called for Simone, and nothing would ever be the same again.

The Awakening

Yessin stared into the fires at the temple complex. The sky above burned brightly with thousands of starlights gazing down at the world below, passing judgement on the lives of the mere mortals beneath them. Yessin, however, knew different; he was no mortal. He had a direct connection with the Hathanoi, a connection that had taken years of dedication to build and nurture, and one that he would protect at all costs.

The fires seemed to burn brighter tonight, seemed to glimmer with a fiercer intensity. Yessin had foreseen this moment many centuries past. He knew that if he missed his moment tonight, he would never get another chance like this.

He turned his attention to the sleeping city beneath him. A small grin passed over his smooth features and passed into his eyes, which appeared to gleam in the snaking embers of the fire. Tonight, one of the Hathoni would awaken that which was dear to him, that which would eventually belong to him... That which he could use to completely control both his own destiny and that of the entire city. The years of waiting would finally be over; all he needed to do now was to discover the chosen person. If they belonged to the lower Hathoni, his task would be much easier. He knew that destiny had an ironic misplaced sense of equality in judgement, that would hopefully ensure that his next task would be easy to accomplish.

He turned his back on the temple doors and walked into the interior of the complex, his long ceremonial shroud rippling in the breeze that he created with each step. He could walk these corridors with ease; he no longer needed to follow the small dimples in the ground that changed in shape depending on which area of the temple the walker wished to visit.

He remembered with fondness his first few years in this, then unfamiliar, building. The excitement with which he had first entered its longed for confines, the joy of discovering exotic and unimaginable rituals and opening his mind to secrets that he thought he'd never be privy to. That had, however, been aeons ago. He had left and returned more times than he could imagine, but each time he left it had been harder to stay away, harder to make the trek into the unknown – so much so that during his last visit he had decided to stay, to finally make the temple his home once again.

Yessin's musings had taken him back to his chambers. He carefully closed the solid wooden door behind him and moved slowly towards his resting place. The Elders took vows of abstinence in all forms. Yessin's chambers were therefore sparsely furnished, but he knew that if his plans came to fruition, then a lot of customs and ideas that were accepted by both the Elders and the Hathoni would soon be changing beyond recognition.

With this final thought pervading his mind, Yessin settled himself onto the cold, stone slab and began his dream sequence, aware that upon awakening, Hathonia would be a different world.

The Search

They stared into the dying embers, the words of the voice haunting their thoughts. Simone had always been told that this moment would arrive. That she, and she alone, was destined to convey the voices of the Shadowlands to the Hathoni, but the moment had arrived and she had not responded. Her training had failed her, instead fear and disbelief had taken its place. Had her moment gone? Had she failed the fallen? Questions fought for attention in her mind, and yet she didn't have any answers.

Alexis sighed beside her.

'So... what now?'

Another question, but at least she knew how to respond to this.

'We must reach the story keeper before the start of the new day.'

'Break curfew? The risks are too many, and you know the punishment if we're caught. We will wait until the next meeting; the threat to your safety if we go now is too great. You know this, Simone.'

'Yes,' she sighed. 'I know all of that, but this is my destiny; it's the reason why we were paired together, for my protection. If we fail to allow the secrets of the Shadowlands to be passed on, all will be lost. I will not let that happen. We must leave now, we have no choice.'

Yessin awoke, the feelings of triumph already flooding through his refreshed body. He dressed quickly and, with a practiced air, soundlessly opened the chamber door. The feeble first rays of sun trickled their way through the maze of corridors. Yessin followed their lines, heading towards their source and a new day.

He knew time was of the essence, the first day of contact would be the most important. The chosen Hathanoi would be unsure of how to act. If he could intercept them and pose as the story keeper, then he would have the power to control their actions.

Quickly he made his way down the steep temple steps and into the sleeping city below, his thoughts following him as he snaked his way through the streets towards the story keeper's lodgings.

Alexis and Simone continued their furtive scurry through the narrow streets of Hathoni, pausing only to check that they hadn't been followed. At one corner, their shadows appeared to scout out the way ahead, aiding their progress and giving them confidence.

'Simone, we're nearly there. When did you last see the story keeper? Will they know why you've arrived?'

She silently nodded her reply.

'I haven't seen them since I was young, but the story keeper will be aware of our arrival tonight. They will have seen it in the scrolls and the stars. Our lives are already mapped until this point. After this, only the shadows know.'

Yessin crept into the story keeper's quarters. The old man was waiting for him.

'I know why you have come.'

'Then you must also know what I have come to do.'

'Indeed.'

'You could have left. Why did you stay? If you knew what my intentions were, why did you choose to remain here?'

'My fate has been sealed in the scrolls and stars for millennia, my personal wishes are of no consequence.'

'Surely you know that fate can be altered, that it is not set in stone? If it were, then how come I am here? I am about to change the chosen one's destiny.'

The story keeper snorted in derision at Yessin's statement.

'Oh Elder, you are still so young in your understanding of our world. One day you will realise that choice is of no consequence. Our lives are mapped out before we even begin – how else would I have known of your arrival?'

Yessin said nothing. The old man's comments disturbed him, and yet he still had to know.

'Tell me, then, before I carry out my destiny – will I succeed?'

'Mine is not to tell of personal gain, just to know the passing of what must be. Your path will always lead you to your destiny, but it is up to you to ensure you get there.'

As the story keeper made his final comment, he knelt in front of Yessin. The Elder raised his ceremonial dagger and slipped it neatly around the old man's neck. Without a sound, he slumped to the floor. Yessin took hold of the story keeper's body and moved him into a recessed corner, murmuring rituals over the corpse as it passed over into the Shadowlands.

He next took up the bloodstained rug and placed it roughly into the corner, after using it to first clean his crimson knife.

Yessin surveyed his new quarters and a satisfied smile eased itself around his lips. He couldn't believe how easy it had been. The story keeper's remarks still bothered him, but as he settled his mind to preparing for the arrival of the chosen one, those doubts soon disappeared.

The Story Keeper

Alexis and Simone waited in the alley across from the story keeper's quarters. They needed to make sure that they hadn't been followed, and that they wouldn't be caught before they completed the final stage of their journey.

Alexis whispered to Simone, 'I'll check to ensure the way is clear. If it is, then come through with me. If anything happens to me, do not under any circumstances try to help me. You are far too important. If I am taken, you must return immediately to our quarters and continue with your day as normal. Inform the meeting council, and rely on their guidance to see you through.'

Simone nodded and gave Alexis' arm a comforting squeeze; he released himself from her and quickly dashed across to the story keeper's door, keeping his hood up as he knocked the required three times.

Nothing happened.

He hadn't counted on what to do if the story keeper didn't reply. Alexis glanced around. By the position of the sun he knew that they still had an hour of curfew to go before they should be seen outside. He was just about to turn and head back towards Simone in the shadows, when the door opened up slightly.

A powerfully built man with a shaved head stared into his eyes.

'I've been waiting for you; what kept you so long?'

Alexis forgot his imminent danger at being exposed and stammered, 'We came as quickly as we could. We are sorry for the delay.'

'We?' the story keeper replied with obvious confusion. 'Where is the other that you speak of?'

Alexis turned and beckoned Simone through from the alley. Yessin watched her furtive approach with hungry eyes. He knew that this was the chosen one. He'd been disappointed when he'd seen the man arrive, as he hadn't lived up to his expectations... But the girl, she was different. He knew he could convince her, use her and bend her wishes to his will.

Simone looked at the tall, powerful man in front of her. She paused; he didn't fit into her memories of the story keeper. She thought he should be small, kindly and wizened, with the memories and knowledge of the ages. Not this athletic giant who stood gleaming in front of her as the first rays of sunlight touched his chiselled scalp. His eyes seemed to bore into hers, they almost looked predatory. He must have sensed her hesitation for he pulled back into the confines of his quarters and seemed to lower his gaze.

'I'm sorry for my impudence, my lady,' Yessin grovelled 'It's just I've been waiting for this moment for so long, that to actually see you at my door stunned me. Please forgive me for staring.'

Yessin hated being subservient to anyone, but he knew that if he was to win this woman over, he had to beg for her forgiveness. He'd noted the fear that he'd seen in her eyes when she first looked on him. He cursed himself for being so stupid, of course she'd have met with the story keeper when she was young; he needed to think fast to offer an excuse for his much changed appearance.

'Please come in. I can hear the sound of the early morning footfalls of the curfew patrol, we mustn't be caught.'

This comment appeared to work perfectly; the skittish couple swiftly entered the deceased story keeper's quarters and walked unknowingly straight into Yessin's control.

Revelations

He ushered them towards the low bench in the corner of the room. The gloom made uneasy shadows across the floor. Yessin knew the customs of the story keepers well, for it was he who had moulded their beliefs, their ideas and stories.

'Please, partake in a cup for the Elders.' He proffered the small wooden bowl towards them.

As was custom Alexis took the cup first, slowing imbibing the rich, sweet flavours before passing it on to Simone. She hesitated before drinking. The look in the man's eyes still disturbed her; he seemed almost desperate for her to take some of the liquid.

'Simone, you need to take the offering for the Elders' sake,' murmured Alexis in her ear. 'We can't afford to offend them now; we need all the help we can get'.

Putting her cautions aside, Simone drank softly from the cup, and passed it on to the story keeper. He drank deeply from it, knowing that when he finished the cup he had forever linked the three of them to each other. It was an old spell, from the beginnings of civilisation, but it worked well and was unbreakable. Something that he needed now to ensure that, no matter what happened, he would always be able to find this one Hathoni and her loyal protector.

'So,' sighed Simone. 'You know why we are here. I missed my opportunity. They got in contact and I failed to fulfil my duty... I let everyone down.'

She started to tremble. Alexis put his arm around her shoulders.

'You've done nothing wrong. You are the chosen one, and that is a huge responsibility. You must have known that you couldn't fulfil your task without my aid. That is, after all, why you have come here so soon after the event... I mean, you broke curfew. Surely that proves to you that you are worthy and strong enough to complete this task?'

Yessin smiled as he saw the effect his words had on Simone. She straightened up, her eyes took on a sheen of resolution, and she appeared to take strength from what he had said. She had given away her weakness – she needed encouragement, constant affirmation that what she was doing was right. That was how he could mould her, bend her to his will, and use her.

'Now, we must discuss how to progress from this point. You need to tell me exactly what happened to bring you here to me this early morning, and it needs to be quick to ensure you are not missed from your morning duties.'

Simone and Alexis proceeded to tell Yessin about the voice, the flaring of the fire and the feeling that they had missed a momentous moment to affect a change for Hathonia.

All the while, the impostor story keeper nodded and listened to their tale, becoming more interested when they spoke of the moment the fires grew brighter. So that was how she was doing it, he mused. He always wondered how she was able to get messages across the void to the numerous 'chosen ones', but he'd never realised just how simple it had been until now.

Simone noticed the smile that eased across the story keeper's face as her tale came to an end. She still felt uneasy around him, and the image she had of the kindly, old man still fought against the reality of the person in front of her.

'Tell me, where is the story keeper that I met many years ago? What happened to him?'

Without hesitating, Yessin explained the ritual of passing down the title of story keeper over the years. He likened it to the role of the Elders, but with the stories passed down through oral tradition, rather than via scribes over many, many years. He reminisced about his training in the arena of souls, and spoke fondly of his growing understanding of the history of Hathonia, and the way that the Hathoni people interconnected over the centuries with their ancestors.

As Simone listened, she found herself softening to this story teller, believing in his passion for the tales of their people. As he began to explain the role of the chosen one, she actually felt herself move forward on the bench.

'The chosen one comes around every few hundred years, when the people of Hathonia are in dire need of a saviour. They can be from any part of the society, male or female. Some are old, and some are – like you were – very young. The story keeper's role is to make sure that they fulfil their destiny... Whatever that may be. In the past, the chosen ones have helped the city to rise up against invaders...'

'Like Altora did with the Yetheni in H21,' chipped in Alexis.

'Yes, exactly like Altora,' Yessin agreed. 'Although that was many centuries past. However, it happened, whatever the threat to our great nation. The chosen ones and the story tellers always did their best to ensure that the city and the people survived.'

'Why now?' Simone interjected. 'Why me?'

'We may never know why you have been chosen to take on this auspicious role. Some chosen ones are never activated; they live out their entire lives never being called upon by the shadows, but we do know the reason why you have been brought to your calling.'

Simone strained further forward, her entire being centred on this one moment of revelation.

'You have been contacted by the land beyond the shadows to free the Hathoni from the shadow keepers themselves.'

There was a stunned silence in the room. Alexis grabbed Simone's shoulder and absentmindedly gripped her purple scarf, twisting the material between his fingers. Simone looked dejectedly at the floor, plaiting her fingers together, unable to process the enormity of the task that lay ahead of her.

'How... I don't understand... Surely that's impossible... How can you say that, that is my task, you must be mistaken.'

'I am not. It is written in the stars that one day a Hathoni will rise to defeat the shadow keepers themselves. They will change the very fabric of Hathonia's society; they will make the Hathoni free.'

Simone stared blankly at the story keeper.

'You are the greatest gift our society has ever had, Simone. You have no idea just how important your existence is, but the time has come for you to leave now.'

'Leave? How can I leave after what you've just told me?'

'Simone,' said Alexis, 'he's right. If we don't leave now, we'll draw attention to ourselves... We must return to our quarters and duties for the day.'

'When will I see you again? When will I learn more of my destiny?'

'All in good time, Simone. I shall contact you.'

He slowly opened the door and checked it was clear, before ushering them on their way. Simone looked back to see the door slowly closing, and as she hurried away by Alexis' side, she realised that no previous meeting had ever changed her as much as that short one had. She, the chosen one, the defeater of the shadow keepers... It was too much to take in.

Yessin waited until he was sure they were far away from the story keeper's hut. He then made a mental note to arrange a sweep-up party to clear up the mess of the old story keeper's body, and then furtively sidled away from the hovel, heading once more for the temple on the hill.

Contact

Simone bent her head against the icy blast that rolled down from the hills above the fields. A week had passed since her meeting with the story keeper, and she still couldn't quite believe the task that had been set for her.

To any casual observer, she was working hard. Her hanodi kept turning the soil in front of her, ensuring that she was preparing the ground for the seeds to be planted. To any of the wardens happening to glance in her direction, she would have seemed the perfect Hathoni worker; purple scarf tightly secured under her Horthari work cap, mind set on the task, working to ensure the survival of the Hathoni people for another harsh winter.

Simone's mind was in turmoil, though. She kept turning over the words she'd been told: 'You have been contacted by the land beyond the shadows to free the Hathoni from the shadow keepers themselves.' She snorted out loud at the ridiculous concept of her, a lowly worker, being able to change the way that they had lived for generations, to free everyone from the fear of the shadow keepers – to cheat death itself. A nearby worker glanced in her direction at the unnatural sound. Simone realised she hadn't internalised her contemptuous derision. She quickly glanced around to look for the telltale signs of frost easing their way towards her, but this time she had escaped unnoticed. She knew she must be more careful in future; any inappropriate noise whilst in the field, could earn the maker a one-way ticket to the land of the shadows.

The piercing end of toil whistle fractured her thoughts, and like the hundreds of other Hathoni workers, Simone gathered up her tools and began the slow procession back to Hathonia, under the ever watchful eyes of the wardens.

As she passed through the outer city wall, the usual feeling of calm worked its way through her. She lifted her head to try to spot Alexis in his usual spot on the viewing platform, but for some reason, today he was not there. Simone instantly stiffened; he was always there, always there to check she got back in safely. She'd never had to worry about him before, never let the thought cross his mind that he was in any danger safely behind the city walls. The shadow keepers never crossed the threshold – well, not in living memory anyway. They always existed beyond the boundary, and in the fields. Not here in the city.

Simone tried to get her thoughts in order. Her worries about the shadow keepers were pointless. He must just be held up somewhere. The more she repeated this to herself, the harder it became to believe.

She handed in her hanodi and got her name signed off quickly. Then began the struggle to get back to their quarters without running – for this was forbidden – through the massive crowds of post-work Hathoni heading for their own dwellings. She eventually made it back, after an inordinate amount of time spent twisting and dodging through the crowds. She wrenched open the door to find Alexis sat crumpled in the corner, the dying embers of a fire flickering in front of his ruined face.

'Alexis!' she screamed as she rushed towards him.

'Please, don't come near me.'

The words seemed to fall out of him as though they came from somewhere else. His one hand feebly held up in front of him to ward off her advances, the other clutched about his feverish chest, desperately pulling the sodden clothing from about him.

She stopped. 'What is it? What's happened to you?'

'Slow plague,' he murmured. 'Leave me'.

Simone sprang backwards from him as though he had just punched her.

'Slow plague... That's impossible... How? Who from?' she continued, backing towards the door, her hand fumbling for the handle.

'I'll be back... with help... I promise.'

She ran from the dwelling, blindly, not caring for any rules, just knowing that she had to get him help.

She turned a corner, rushing for the council, and hit a solid wall of towering muscle. Strong arms grasped her. She twisted in fear away from them, desperate to get help for Alexis.

'Stop your struggling, child; you don't need to struggle anymore.'

Simone slowly turned her tear-stained eyes up to meet the eyes of the story keeper. She sobbed into his chest.

'He's being taken from me!'

'My dear, I know – that's why I came. Already I have the health keepers on their way to aid your protector.'

'Y… you know? But I only just found out... How can you know?!'

'As soon as you came to my door, you connected us all together. The stars foretold of this tragic moment. I came as soon as I could. I'm sorry it couldn't have been sooner.'

'Will he survive?'

'Only time will tell, my dear.'

'Where will he be taken?'

'To the healing quarter. He'll be well looked after, and as soon as he is safe and well, we'll be able to visit him again.'

Simone realised that she was still holding onto his arms, and that her tears had soaked through his robes.

'I'm so sorry, I just...'

'My dear, do not concern yourself,' he murmured as he disentangled himself from her. 'Now, we must get you somewhere safe to discuss your own future. With your protector away we must decide upon a plan for you.'

With those words, Yessin led her away from her quarter towards the temple district. Simone was so exhausted from her recent ordeal that she let him lead the way, not noticing where he was taking her.

Retraining

Simone awoke, feeling the unfamiliar sensation of stiffness spreading through her back and neck. Rubbing her tired limbs she surveyed her surroundings. The room was small, and the pain in her body could now be traced to the flat stone slab she had spent the night on. No wonder she ached all over – how could anyone lie on that, let alone sleep? And yet she had. Had she really been so tired? Obviously, if she had survived a night on that, and yet she had no memory of getting here... She remembered meeting the story keeper, and the pain of seeing Alexis suffer from the slow plague, but of her journey here she had no memory.

Slowly, she made her way from the stone resting place towards the only source of light; a small window at the opposite side of the room. The events of the previous day played back through her mind. She struggled to find any memory of how she had reached her current situation. A small sob escaped her lips as she remembered the sight of Alexis, his outstretched hand warning her away from him.

She used the windowsill to pull her sore body upwards, her mind still fumbling with the details of the loss of her protector. She wondered where he was. The healing quarter was out of bounds to healthy Hathoni. The only way she'd see him now was when, and if, he got better. Even then though she knew they wouldn't be able to stay in the same quarter together, the rules of Hathonia stated that once a citizen had been released from the healing quarter, they had to remain in the convalescing quarter for a further year, to ensure control over spreading diseases.

With these thoughts trickling through her mind, a sudden thrill of panic coursed throughout her body as she realised where she had spent the night. The view spreading out beneath the window could only be seen from one place in the whole of Hathonia – the temple.

All pain dissipated from her as the fear flooded through her veins. She sprinted to the solid wooden door and struggled fruitlessly to open it. Time and again she slammed her small frame up against the solid barrier, trying desperately to break through it to escape from the confines of her prison. She shouted for her release until her voice had left her and eventually, as the sun began to once again sink below the horizon, sending soft shadows dancing across the cell, she slumped exhausted to the floor to await her fate.

Yessin had sat quietly all afternoon, listening to the muffled thumps and shouts emanating from behind the door. He waited for them to stop – patience had been at the forefront of his training – and eventually, after the sounds had waned, he walked slowly towards the central atrium to the weekly evening meeting of the chief Elders.

As he walked, he considered his plan of action. The easy part had been getting the girl into the temple. It had been hard ensuring that the boy contracted the slow plague, but the reaction from Simone was exactly what he'd wanted; she'd come with him so easily, he'd almost been surprised by her compliance. He had expected more of the scene that had been demonstrated today, but at least she had been in a locked room without an audience, a difficult incident had been avoided – and hopefully that would make his next task a little easier.

The chief Elders had gathered around the central atrium, the fire burning in the middle casting out the shadows and throwing a warm glow over the gathered faces that shimmered every time the breeze sauntered through their sacred confines. The elements were respected by the Elders and allowed to work as they pleased. In exchange, the Elders were able to call on them in times of great need to assist in any way that they could. In the past, a severe drought had been averted when the ancient grand Elder Athoria had called upon the water elements to aid their plight. In return, they had ensured that the citizens of Hathonia would not harness the power of the Hadoria River for their own gain – an uneasy truce that still existed to this day.

The current grand Elder, Axoria, stood directly in the central point of the atrium, with the fire off to his right. This was the point of greatest power in the entire temple, and Yessin coveted this position.

'Ah, Grand Advisor... You've arrived!'

Axoria was able to silence a room with only a few words, and with these the previous mutterings washed away into nothing.

'Apologies for my late arrival, Axoria. I was detained on a serious matter of which I would like to speak with all of you about.'

'The time for speaking will come after the usual ceremonies, Yessin... Please take your place in the round.'

'Yes, Grand Elder,' intoned Yessin as he hurriedly slotted into his accustomed space. He fixed his face into a look of reverence. He knew his time would soon be here, and he could little afford to lose the respect of the other Elders by forcing Axoria to hear his point now. Presently he would be standing in the central spot, and when that happened, an awful lot of other things would change.

Simone slowly pulled herself up off the cold floor. The sun had completely disappeared from view, and the silvery moon had replaced her orbit. The door was still shut, and nothing in the room had changed, apart from the length of the shadows. She sighed and moved over to the stone slab, stretching and pulling her arms about her, trying desperately to get some warmth into her upper body. A thin blanket lay at the end of the slab. It wouldn't provide much heat, but at least it would be something. She perched herself on the edge of the stone and wrapped herself in the pale blue cover, and once again waited for fate to dictate her future.

Yessin repeated the ancient words of the Elders whilst passing the cup of faith onto the Elder on his right. The drone of the creed echoed around the circular chamber. The words were older than the Temple itself, and acted as the force that bound the Elders to each other and the surrounding elements. Each Elder learnt the creed's words as part of their first test, and they were emblazoned above the inner temple sanctum's door as a constant reminder to 'free your mind, to free the people, to free Hathonia, to free yourself.'

The cup of faith completed its circle and came to a rest in the Grand Elder's hand. Axoria raised the cup above his head and said the closing words of the ceremony.

'We, the faithful, are all now bound in our quest for freedom. May the Hathanoi bless our efforts and grant us the wisdom to see the truth, hear the righteous and speak our knowledge to free us all.'

'We agree to serve in order to gain freedom,' came the reply from the gathered Elders.

The ceremonial aspect of the meeting over, the Elders were now free to wander around the chamber and to converse freely.

Yessin approached Axoria.

'Grand Elder,' he whispered as he stepped slowly to Axoria's side. 'I need to bring a matter of great importance to your notice.'

'Not now, Yessin. You can bring your matter to me at the normal appointed hour tomorrow.'

'But Axoria, this matter cannot wait any longer.'

'Yessin, it must,' said Axoria as he walked away from him.

Yessin could wait no longer. 'I've found her,' he shouted across the chamber 'I've found the chosen one.'

All talk ceased, an eerie hush descended across the atrium. The Elders seemed to turn as one towards Yessin, and the shock of his disclosure reverberated around them all.

'What, do you mean, you've found her?' queried Axoria.

'I mean to say that the chosen one, the one who heard the voice beyond the Shadows, is here. I have her in a chamber within the temple complex.'

'Why did you not tell me as soon as she arrived here? You know how important the chosen one is. Any delay in giving her the knowledge she needs will mean a delay in getting the message across from the land beyond the shadows.'

Yessin patiently replied, 'If you remember, Grand Elder, I tried, and you did not listen.'

A palpable whisper echoed around the Elders. Yessin knew he had played the moment perfectly; Simone would be accepted as an Elder without question now, as Axoria tried to make up for his previous error.

'Yessin, what has happened is in the past now – it is the future we must look to. Bring her to me.'

'I will, on one condition... That she is named as an Elder.'

An intake of breath met this statement, but Yessin knew that there could only be one answer.

Axoria sighed. 'Yes,' he whispered, knowing that with that one syllable he had sealed the end of his own reign as Grand Elder.

Revelation

Simone moved cautiously further back onto the slab at the first sound of the key turning in the door. She wrapped the blanket further round herself, knowing that it offered no protection from whatever lay beyond the door, but the warmth somehow made her feel more secure.

The door slowly inched open to reveal a small, wizened man with a tray of food and a pitcher of water balanced carefully on one hand. In the other a key, presumably to her cell, dangled from a long length of rope.

'I'm so sorry to keep you waiting, Simone. You have no idea how long we've waited to meet you. The delay in coming to you is inexcusable on our part, and we can only apologise. Please, eat, drink… All of your questions will be answered when you are rested.'

With that, he placed the tray onto the floor, and disappeared, shutting and locking the door behind him.

Simone waited until the bolt clunked into place before slowly sliding off the stone slab. The tray and the food upon it looked so inviting, but at the back of her mind was the nagging fear that they had tampered with it. Her stomach growled its presence and, throwing caution to the wind, she delved in.

Hours passed, and the night started to creep back into the chamber. Still nothing happened. She'd eaten the food, slept, awoken and waited… For what, she wasn't sure. As she began to consider the possibility of sleep once again, a soft click heralded the key turning in the lock. There was a pause before the door slowly swung inwards; a soft glow illuminated the shadows of the men behind the threshold. Her eyes struggled to adjust to the influx of light in her dull chamber. Then, from out of the shadows, she heard the voice she'd been dreading.

'Simone, welcome, your journey is complete. You are home.'

Simone's confusion erupted into anger as she saw the hateful figure of Yessin waver in the firelight.

'Home? How can I be home? You took my home from me... You kidnapped me, imprisoned me, removed my rights and freedom – and yet you say I am home... How dare you insult me!'

He walked in towards her, hands up in protest, trying to deflect the vicious words from his presence.

'Simone, I know we haven't treated you in the best manner, but please believe me when I say you are home. We have waited so long to be in the presence of the Chosen One that when the momentous occasion arrived, we did not know how to behave... As such we can only apologise.'

Simone looked from Yessin to the other Elders in disbelief.

'But you were my story keeper, we trusted you... And now I'm here, in the temple.'

She sat back down on the stone slab, the confusion keeping her from remaining upright. 'I just, I... Ugh... I don't understand.'

'Soon, my dear Simone, you will. Please, come with us – we have a special quarter made up for you, one that will befit your station... One that will allow you to roam the temple without impediment.'

Not knowing how to remove herself from her current predicament, Simone reluctantly followed the Elders, Yessin once again guiding her by the arm.

Quarantine

Alexis groaned in discomfort as he slowly shifted position in his bed. The worst of the fever was over, but he still suffered from aches and pains. Many a night the nurses had had to wake him as he struggled to gain his bearings, and called out time and time again for Simone to rescue him. They said that he was 'delirious', and that he should focus on the here and now rather than the past. He always refused to agree with them. As far as he saw it, Simone was the present and the future, and he could not just relegate her to the past. That, for him, was the only thing that would ensure that he got better.

As time went on, he began to take more notice of his surroundings. The ward he had been transferred into seemed to hold all of the Hathoni, who were improving in their conditions – a fact that once he realised, he was extremely grateful of. The walls were a pallid grey and the health workers bustled around noiselessly, first tending to one patient, and then another.

As Alexis' health improved, memories of the night he was transferred into quarantine slowly came back to him. There had been a tall man, and some words, and a strange light. The more he tried to focus on the memory, the further it seemed to distort, as though it was some shy animal avoiding capture.

The odd semi-life continued. He ate, drank, did his exercises, and spoke to the health workers and the other patients. Occasionally he got to walk outside for a few brief moments, but on the whole, he lay there. Lay looking up at the grey ceiling, thinking of Simone and trying to remember how he had ended up in such a place.

One evening, as he lay watching the light fade from the room, he started to remember the build up to the evening when his life had been emptied of Simone. He had been sitting on the floor, starting to prepare the evening dinner, and readying himself for his usual sprint to the top of the wall to watch her enter the confines of the city limits, when a shadow fell and grew slowly into the room. He'd looked up and watched the outline of the story keeper slowly work his way into their quarters.

He'd remembered being startled about the surreptitious invasion, and asking why the story keeper had made his way down to the workers' quarter. The story keeper hadn't answered, and just continued to walk forward. At this point Alexis had become scared, worried about the story keeper's intentions. Just as he began to wonder whether he should try to leave, he felt a strange pain in his arm and heard some odd words being spoken over him. He remembered looking up, and seeing the hatred on the story keeper's face, and then darkness overtook him.

Alexis sat up with a jolt. He started throwing off his cover and began to walk, unsteadily at first, and then moving with greater speed towards the exit door. Health workers tried to stand in his way, but his need to get to Simone, to let her know what he now knew, was far greater, and he knew he could stand up to any obstacles they threw into his path.

His only goal was escape, to get her to safety. To ensure the story keeper didn't cause any more harm.

Initiation

Simone stood in the candlelit room. Her blue robe with the white crest of the Elders emblazoned on the chest billowed in the cool breeze from the open windows. She had to admit to herself that even though she was uneasy, a strange feeling of calm was beginning to work its way into her system.

The panic of the first few days of isolation began to ease when she realised that she wasn't going to be harmed by the Elders. The days that followed the reunion with her story teller had been interesting ones. Yessin had explained to her that he had had to disguise himself to gain her trust and confidence. He informed her in his smooth, calm voice that if he'd taken her straight from her quarter to the temple she would have panicked so badly that it would have interrupted her link with the Shadowlands, something that they could ill afford to do, and so it was agreed amongst the Elders that he, Yessin, would gain access to her world through deceitful means.

This seemed to make sense to Simone. She had at first questioned why the Elders could not disclose their true intentions, but after thinking through Yessin's answers, she began to concede that their strange approach had been the correct one.

The next step had been for her to ask after Alexis. She wanted to visit him, to ensure that he was safe and recovering well. After all, he was her protector, and she knew that she would not be heading towards becoming an Elder without his intervention.

Yessin kept repeating, 'When you are an Elder you will be able to walk freely wherever you please; until then you must remain in our watchful care. There are dark forces at work here that you don't understand, and we cannot let you be exposed to them. Therefore, you are forbidden from leaving the safety of the temple walls.'

Simone hated the idea that Alexis would be out there, alone, unable to know where she was, or what was happening to her. She wanted to find him, and let him know that she was safe, but the idea of being taken by 'dark forces' terrified her. She knew that she would have to wait until the day of her initiation into the way of the Elders. As far as she knew, she was the first female to witness, let alone take part in the ancient ceremony.

The candles flared as the wind teased around the circle, messing about with the robes as it passed through the chamber. Simone was surrounded; her place in the middle of the circle symbolised her respect for the Elders, and her junior position in their ranks. It also allowed the others to move around her, sharing their knowledge and understanding as they paced past her.

At each swing of the temple bell a new Elder appeared in front of her, placed their hands onto her shoulders, stared intently into her eyes and murmured their piece of knowledge, quietly.

Each of the Elders retained a set part of the original scroll of the Elder role – a manuscript written aeons ago, interlaid with the rights of the Elders, their responsibilities for their people and the code of conduct that they all had to adhere to. At each initiation, this knowledge passed on to the new Elder, and with the eventual passing of an ancient Elder, the new initiate would take on their information in preparation to pass it on. By doing this, all of the Elders were able to take responsibility for their own history.

Simone soaked up the history of the Elders; by the end of the 'passing' she accepted her new role by repeating the words that had been whispered to her.

'I, Simone, new initiate into the ways of the Elders, do faithfully promise to adhere to the ways of old set down in the Elder role.

'I will ensure that the rights of others are met above my own, that all civilians of Hathonia are treated fairly and equally. I will endeavour to uphold the ideals of all Elders, those of tranquillity, knowledge and protection. I know that I must strive for excellence in my studies into the laws, rights and ways of Hathonia. I understand the enormity of the responsibility placed upon me, and the consequences if I fail to abide by these laws. I accept the punishment of "Outlander", and know that if it is given, I will deserve to spend the rest of my days outside of the safety of the walls, without the support of my Elder brothers. This I have said and this I will stand by. Please accept me as not only an Elder, but also a guardian of our great city.'

The Elders nearest to Simone began to blow out their candles, until a widening circle of darkness radiated out away from her. Yessin then lit the central flame, and led the Elders in the acceptance chant.

'We welcome our new Elder sister. We aim to teach her, guide her and envelope her into the ways of the Elders.'

Yessin then stepped forward and spoke alone.

'Simone, we accept you into our fold. As one of the spiritual guiders of this great city, you now have a huge responsibility to fulfil. Your duties will commence tomorrow, but for the moment, Sister – we celebrate your new role.'

Simone's smile spread slowly across her face.

'Thank you my brothers,' she managed to murmur through the tears of happiness that slowly slid down her cheeks.

She finally felt as though she truly belonged somewhere, and the relief that they had accepted her overwhelmed her senses, as she dissolved into their arms and accepted the wine and food that they offered her in celebration of her achievement.

First Steps

Yessin had retired to his quarters early. He wanted Simone to enjoy the celebrations, and he knew that she would only do that if he absented himself. He was happy to do so. The strain of the last few days was starting to tell, and he needed to be composed if he was to complete his transformation into the Grand Elder. Axoria had shown himself to be a weak leader and, with the initiation of Simone, Yessin was one step closer to becoming the new leader of the Elders.

He knew that Axoria was respected by the other Elders, but then he also knew that doubts about his control over the civilians of Hathonia had started to creep in. The other Elders wanted to know how he had missed Simone's awakening as a viable link between this world and the Shadowlands. How was it that Yessin, an otherwise unassuming advisor to the Elders, had found her, brought her into their fold and then protected her completely by making her into an Elder? Yes, Yessin smiled, his time was indeed almost upon him. He just had to ensure that Simone stayed on side and didn't cause any issues for him. Having Alexis confined to the healing quarter was – he had to admit to himself – a stroke of genius. It meant that Simone was now completely in his power. He smiled about how readily she'd accepted that there were 'dark forces' at work... Little did she know that they were already inside the temple walls, ready to pounce on his command, her idea of safety had already been compromised.

Alexis sat with his back against the cool wall; the last few hours had passed in a blur. How he'd managed to muster the strength to get past the health workers he would never know, but he'd done it. He'd managed to escape, to get out of the healing quarter, but as his breathing slowed to a controllable rate, he realised that he had a daunting task in front of him to ensure that he could actually reach Simone.

His first obstacle would be to gain new clothes. He was currently wearing the robes of the healing quarter. If he was caught by the guards, no amount of explaining would excuse his attire, and all his efforts to free himself would have been in vain.

After that, he would then need to work his way back to his own quarter, and try to work out where Simone was, and what had happened to her.

Simone, meanwhile, was completely oblivious to the danger that had enveloped her. She slowly edged her way back towards her room, the wine still eddying around her brain, causing simple steps to become an inhuman feat of endurance.

She was still overwhelmed by the reception she had received – the first female Elder, incredible.

The flickering candlelight of her room welcomed her, and she edged herself into a world of tumultuous dreams.

Plans

The next few weeks passed by in a blur. Simone woke early, passed her meditation hour in the room of reflection, and then broke her fast each morning with the other Elders in the communal room. The rest of her day was filled with inductions into the law of the land, meeting the citizens of Hathonia and aiding them with their many problems and queries. Some of these meetings were easily solved; others, such as difficulties with family interactions, took up more of her time, and had to be handled more delicately.

As Simone grew used to her role, she began to relax, and that's when it started to happen – slowly at first, but then growing in clarity each day... The voices came back. She hadn't realised how much she had missed them, and how much the strain of the past few weeks had stopped her from hearing them, but as they returned, she realised that they had never really been gone – she just hadn't been listening, and for this she cursed herself. The only reason she had become an Elder was due to being the chosen one that the voices had disclosed themselves to, and she had ignored them, too swept along by the importance of herself.

At night she would now sit and clear her mind. She called greatly on the meditation techniques she had learnt whilst in the temple to calm and settle her thoughts from the passing of the day; and as the queries about grazing rights of animals, arguments with siblings and the bustle of the day slipped out of her conscious mind, she heard them.

'Simone. I need you. We need you. We've been left too long in the dark. Our story needs to be told by you. We are suffering, Simone. All of us are suffering. We are drowning in the lands of the shadows, and we cannot breathe.'

Simone gathered her thoughts and sent a single question into the void. 'Why?'

'All is not as it seems, Simone. They are tricking you. They have manipulated us all. They fear us. You must make them see that we are not to be feared. We have done nothing wrong. And yet we are being punished for the deeds of old.'

'I don't understand,' whispered Simone. 'Who is being manipulated? Where are you?'

'We are beyond your help, but others can still be saved. We were taken Simone, taken before all of your eyes. Yet no one reacted. No one helped. They rule by fear. They control through fear. They thrive on our misery. We are in the land of the shadows, and we cannot escape.'

Simone breathed in sharply, she had not realised until then that she had ceased breathing. Tears welled up in her eyes – how could this have happened? These people were innocent, and yet they had been forced into a life of misery, leaving behind their loved ones, forced to spend the rest of eternity in solitude.

'How can I help? What do I need to do?'

'You must make the people understand. The shadows can be beaten...'

A loud knock at the door made Simone jump. The candles streamed back into life as Yessin walked into her room.

'Simone, why are you on the floor? Meditation is not for another hour. Is everything okay?'

'Sorry, Yessin. I wanted to get some more practise before this evening's session. I don't feel that I'm able to make the group connection yet, so I needed to work on clearing my mind.'

'I see... Is that all? There seemed to be a strange energy burst emanating from this room... You know that you need to contact me straight away the minute they start communicating with you again.'

'Energy burst? That's interesting, I didn't feel anything. Are you sure you did?'

'Simone, I am soon to become the Grand Elder, and I would appreciate your honesty in all matters. I don't want to regret my decision to have you initiated into the ways of the Elders.'

Simone paused. She knew that she had to tread carefully to remain undiscovered, but she didn't want to arouse suspicion.

'Yessin, I'm sorry you feel that I am being dishonest in any way, but I want to assure you that as soon as I am contacted, I will inform you first. You are the reason that I've become an Elder, and I cannot let you down.'

Yessin smiled slowly, and turned. As he made his way out the door, he hissed, 'Ensure you don't, Simone. I'm counting on you.'

The door closed and Simone sank onto the stone slab that doubled up as her bed. The enormity of her situation began to dawn on her, and she did not feel comfortable about her position within it. Tomorrow she would go to the quarantine quarter to see Alexis. She missed him, and had not been able to see him until now... However, tomorrow was the first day where she was to be granted leave from the temple, and she couldn't wait to see her protector again.

Hathonia

Simone stepped out into the warm sunlight, and breathed in. The smell of corn, laundry, bread and dust washed over her senses. The warmth of her smile hit the citizens, standing and waiting to enter the temple. All who saw it knew that she was glad to be alive, and to be standing on that very spot.

Simone almost ran down the temple steps. She couldn't believe that they had kept to their word and let her out into the city. The sun felt good on her skin, the breeze played about her hooded robes, and she felt elated to be 'free'.

The citizens of Hathonia smiled to see the first female Elder looking so relaxed and happy as she moved quickly around the city. She was a welcome break from the stern-faced old men who scowled out at the world from under their protective cowls. They returned her wishes of health and happiness as she moved through each of the quarters, making her way towards the quarantine area.

Simone paused under the motto of Hathonia, reminding all who entered the quarantine area to 'clean, cleanse and strengthen' their resolve to gain their health again.

Simone couldn't wait to see Alexis again. She walked with purpose up towards the quarantine Sister to state her intentions, but before she could even speak the sister took her arm, and whilst leading her away from the entrance stated, 'My apologies, but even as an Elder you must abide by our strict infection control rules. Visitors are not allowed into the quarantine area, if the person you wish to visit gains their health again, then by all means you are more than welcome to visit them in the health quarter... But until that time, I'm afraid you must stay away.'

Simone's heart sank. All she wanted was to see her Alexis, but the Sister had refused her entry, and had managed to walk her away from the quarter's entrance whilst speaking with her.

Simone stood, tears massing in her eyes as she watched the retreating back of the Sister disappear into the quarter, the metal gates closing slowly behind her. Simone turned and, determined not to return to the temple until her curfew, began to make her way back to her old quarter to see her lodgings for the last time before the opportunity passed her by.

Simone paused outside the door of her lodgings. The ground outside had been recently disturbed and fresh footprints lay in the dust. She hesitated. Had they re-let the room? Surely they knew that both she and Alexis intended to keep the place, even if it would just be somewhere for Alexis to live in once he had recovered from his illness.

Alexis stood behind the door, a broken chair leg raised above his head. He had heard the strange noises outside the door, and was determined not to be taken again. Not now that he was on the mend and starting to feel close to recovery, starting to feel close to being ready to find Simone and leave this place they had once called 'home'.

Simone gently pushed open the door, slowly.

'Hello? Is there anybody here? I don't mean to disturb you, but this is still really my old home...'

She felt a hand grab her, then another and before she could let out a scream, or try to pull free, the door had shut, and she was being pulled in towards a faintly familiar person. As they hugged her, her mind conflicted between knowing and sensing it was Alexis, and disbelieving that it could be. Only when he let her out of his vice-like grasp could she splutter her incredulity that it was actually him.

'Alexis, here, how... I don't understand! I thought you were in quarantine!?'

'Oh Simone, I was, but I managed to escape. I can't believe you're here... I thought it was them, come to take me away from you again!'

He paused, looked at her, and said, 'What are you wearing? Did you rob an Elder on the way here? I've been so worried about you.'

'What do you mean, escape and taken? Alexis, you're frightening me. What happened to you?'

'Sit down. I'll secure the door, and then we can exchange our stories...'

Simone did as he asked, and within the hour – punctuated by many gasps of horror, and tears of frustration – they both knew the other's story.

'I can't believe that they took you like that, and tricked me into thinking that I would be helping you by becoming an Elder. I trusted them. How could they?'

'Simone, I've also heard that the body of the story keeper was found the other day, in his lodgings, wrapped in an old rug. We've been played like fools from the very beginning.'

'Why, though? What do we have that they can possibly want?'

'You have us, Simone'

Alexis baulked as the ethereal voices broke into their conversation. Simone remained calm; the voices were now an ever-present bubble of noise in her semi-consciousness now, and so when they broke into audible noise, it didn't shock her as much as it had the first time.

'I don't understand, though – why are you so important?'

'It's not us that are important, Simone – it is you... The fact that you can hear us, and not only that... That you listen to us.'

'Surely there have been others that you have tried to contact, though?'

'Of course, but only a few have heard us, and fewer still have listened. You, Simone, are the only one who will listen, and attempt to do something.'

'Why is Yessin so interested in me, though? He took a huge risk introducing me into the ways of the Elders.'

'He wants the power you wield, Simone. He wants the power to communicate with us in the Shadowlands.'

'Why?' interjected Alexis.

'The ancients believed that if you could communicate with the Shadowlands, you could control not only the order of life after death, but also actual life. If Yessin gains this power from you, he can control who is taken into the Shadowlands. He can decide who lives and who dies. He will control all of Hathonia's fate.'

'That's impossible. If what you're saying is true, then I must already have that power.'

'You do, Simone, but you would never use it to control others. You are far too strong to succumb to that. Yessin is weak – he is ruled by his desire for control, he is greedy and cannot let go of that greed. Simone, you have never had that greed – you do not want for anything, you abhor the suffering of others, and for that you are perfect for our task.'

'What is it that you would have me do?'

'We need you to travel to Yetheni; there they have the power to break the connection with the Shadowlands forever. If you succeed, Hathonia will never be troubled by shadows again.'

'Yetheni? How do they have this power? They are evil – they kill Hathoni for fun.'

'Do they, Simone? Or is that just what you've been told?'

Simone and Alexis looked at one another, and in that instant they both understood the situation in Hathonia.

'For too long the Hathoni have been duped into believing that the Elders are their saviours, that without them they would starve... Simone, you have a chance to stop the shadows, to give Hathonia a chance to be the strong, proud city it used to be.'

As Simone looked into Alexis' eyes, she murmured, 'I accept.'

Preparation

Over the next few days, Simone and Alexis hid within their quarter. They left their own lodgings and stayed hidden with friends. People who understood that something momentous was about to happen, but didn't want to push either of their guests to share that information.

Every day patrols were sent around the city to try to find the missing Elder. Every day Simone and Alexis hid in the readymade fake wall to avoid detection. Sometimes they were sure they were going to be pulled from their hiding area, but as they days wore on, they became more confident that they would remain undetected.

Yessin strode around the temple, barking orders at anyone who stood too near to him. He was furious. His protégée, his one chance at controlling this feckless city, had slipped through his fingers, and he had been too proud, too willing, to believe her, too blind to see that she knew all along his intentions for her.

Simone and Alexis began to prepare their escape. They had provisions to get them through the wasteland, and contacts to help them escape. All they needed to do now was to wait for a moonless night.

The star watcher had predicted one for the next day's hours of darkness, and so they spent the preceding hours sleeping in order to conserve their strength.

Finally a knock at their door roused them from their agitated state of wishful sleep and sent them scuttling for their belongings... The time had come.

Escape

Their guide did not introduce himself, but waited patiently whilst they said their goodbyes, and dressed themselves into their inky black robes. Alexis wound Simone's Horthari cap around her long hair, and smiled encouragingly at her. Then they were out in the night. The clouds enveloped the moon and stopped her silvery beams from giving away their location.

They hurried down winding passages, past sleeping lodgings, over dusty streets always watching their guide, forever heading towards the wall and the next stage of their adventure.

As they neared the wall the presence of the guards increased dramatically. Their guide slowed his pace and motioned for them to dip down towards the ground. They dutifully followed, and progressed slowly for the next six hundred feet on their stomachs, pausing every time their guide raised his hand.

The stone walls towered above their heads. What once had been a welcome sight of protection when returning from a day in the fields, now looked like an insurmountable obstacle; something that would forever keep them from gaining their freedom.

Simone heard the encouraging whispers of the voices as she progressed along. They gave her strength and made her feel as though she could really achieve anything. Alexis' hand on her ankle made her jump, but as he squeezed, she again relaxed. Knowing he was here as well to support her, made the task she had been given far less daunting.

Their guide indicated that they would need to crouch down where he was, and wait quietly for his low call. They would then be able to move quickly and quietly towards the base of the wall for the final climb out.

Crouching down, Simone felt as though hours had passed. She heard some scuffling and a low moan above her, but then all went quiet again. As the minutes passed, her fear of capture grew greater. What if their guide was not who he said he was, and instead led them straight into a trap? What if he himself was caught – what would she and Alexis do then? A low owl hoot disturbed her thoughts; the signal to go had been made. Putting the doubts out of her mind and steeling herself for the run and long climb, she pushed herself away from her hiding space and into the warm night.

The rope felt hard against her hands. The knots were well spaced for a man, but she struggled to pull herself upwards between the big gaps. Their guide was helping her from above and Alexis was steadying her feet from down below, but she still felt very exposed on her long, slow climb upwards.

As the top slowly approached, she began to feel the dull ache that hanging and pulling your own body weight up inflicts upon your arms. As she reached for the next knot on the rope, her hand slipped. She let out a small squeal of terror before the guide grabbed her loose hand and pulled her onto the top of the wall. She was furious with herself, even more so for making the noise. The guide began to scan the walls, looking for guards, and as Simone looked with him, she saw a shadow flicker over the body of a dead guard. Alexis pulled himself up onto the ledge and watched the direction of Simone's wavering hand and terrified eyes.

The shadow was more concerned with the dead body than with the three would-be escapees, but Simone couldn't believe their guide would have put them into such a position. She understood that their escape would be fraught with danger, but to place a dead man so close to their escape route was surely folly. Why had he not moved their rope further away from a possible encounter with a shadow?

The guide motioned for them to be still as he took the rope and lowered it over the other side of the wall. He pointed for Alexis to go down first, in order to help Simone over afterwards. Alexis gave Simone's hand a quick squeeze and then moved out over the edge.

Simone swung her leg to follow after Alexis, but the guide had grabbed her waist stopping her from moving. As he did so, the moon slid out from underneath a cloud, her beam striking the top of the guide's head. Simone gasped in fear as Yessin's smooth features were revealed to her.

'You honestly don't think it would be that easy to escape from me, do you, Simone? You've disappointed me. I asked you if I could trust you, and you promised me that I could... Very upsetting, Simone, and very worrying for you.'

Simone desperately tried to pull away, but his grip remained firm.

'Simone, I'm clear – you can start to come down now,' called Alexis from below.

The shadow started to creep closer, interested in the heightened emotions that presented themselves to it, especially emanating from the girl, it could feel her frustration and loss crackling around the air.

'I won't help you, Yessin. You'll get nothing from me... Nothing at all.'

'Oh, I don't need your help, Simone – just your mind. I can access all I need just by possessing your mind. I have powers that you don't understand, and I shall use them to get what I need from you and Hathonia.'

Simone struggled to pull herself away from Yessin.

'Alexis! Help me!' she cried, as she frantically pushed herself away from her attacker.

As she leant back, her carefully tied Horthari cap began to loosen. She felt it unravelling, but to grasp it would be to allow Yessin to win, for her and Alexis to fail. She witnessed the approach of the shadow from out of her left field of vision.

'Let it go, Simone,' the voices whispered. 'We will catch you.'

Simone made one last desperate push to get away from Yessin, and as she felt the freedom of the air around her, her cap worked its own way to freedom and fell away from her, uncovering her long hair before spiralling away into the breeze and the moonlight.

It all happened so quickly. The frost grew, Yessin desperately tried to regain his balance whilst reaching towards Simone, trying to cover her hair, to save her for himself. Alexis watched, stunned, as the cap fell past him on his reckless climb back up the rope to get to Simone, and the shadow... The shadow gently slipped its hand through Simone's and, without a word, as the world dimmed and diminished around her, carefully carried her off to the Shadowlands.